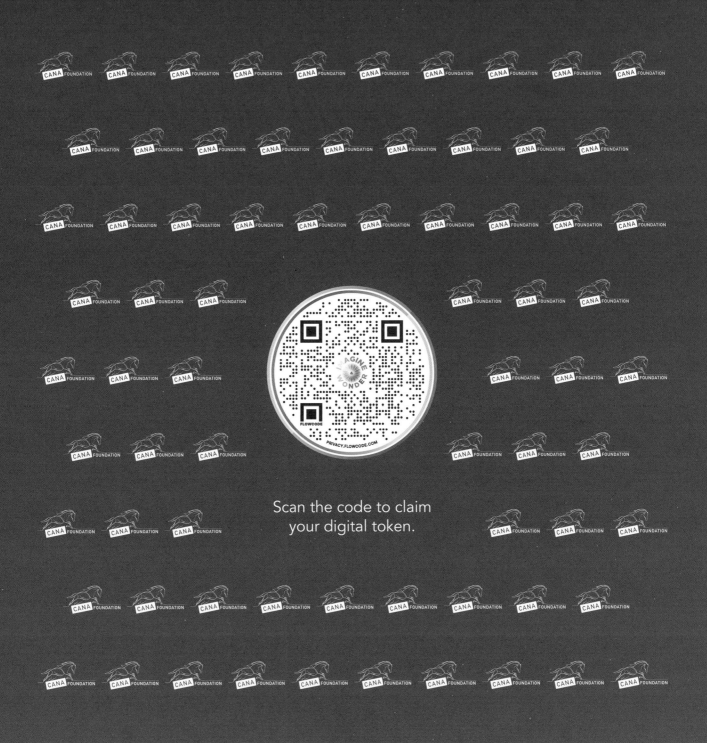

Scan the code to claim
your digital token.

Cello Comes Home

Born to Rewild

Dr. Simon Mills and Dr. Ross MacPhee

This book includes rhyming tools. Scan the code to see how they work.

This book is produced in partnership with

A Brief History of The Horse

The horse—*Equus caballus*—as we know it, is a very recent species that appeared in the last 1 million years or so. It all began with a little guy known as The Dawn Horse or *Hyracotherium* about 50 million years ago, give or take a small horse. That was back in the epoch (period of time) known as the Eocene. This book will explore the modern horse, its current predicament in the United States, and its importance to the subject of rewilding. Below is a representation of some earlier phases of horse evolution and their ages.

Eocene	Oligocene	Miocene	Pliocene	Pleistocene

Hyracotherium (The Dawn Horse)	*Mesohippus*	*Merychippus*	*Dinoohippus*	*Equus caballus*
~50 million years ago	40 million years ago	30 million years ago	5 million years ago	1 million years ago

We are led to believe that a long time ago
something caused horses to get up and go
9000 B.C., they were no more to be?
We'll explore through science and see what we see

Did the land bridge we lost–
keep our horse from our shores?
Did the horses come here with the conquistadors?
Or was the horse that came back the same horse, in fact?
Or did they just never leave? As some people believe

I'm Dr. McCana, and I'm here to explore
Horses, forces, courses, and more
We will learn why "rewilding" has emerged as a word,
and why it's important, from mammals to birds

Rewilding can heal our planet's malaise.
It can neutralize the carbon we produce every day
We'll explore all our options and the options there isn't,
so our species endures like the dinosaurs' didn't

Glossary of terms

Rewilding: conservation efforts aimed at restoring and protecting natural processes and wilderness areas.

Herd: a social group of certain animals of the same species, either wild or domestic.

Nativeness: noun. the quality of belonging to or being connected with a certain place or region by virtue of birth or origin.

Megabeast: any large animal species, especially any weighing 100–10,000 pounds. Almost all megabeasts are extinct.

DNA: deoxyribonucleic acid is a self-replicating material that is present in nearly all organisms as the main constituent of chromosomes. It is the carrier of genetic information.

Now, back to our horses, who once roamed free
The mighty wild mustangs that we used to see
Now kept in cages, considered 'invasive'
But as I explained, they're American natives

If horses could just have their rights reconciled,
they could reclaim their freedom, return to the wild
But it's not just the horses; it's inhabitants all
The land needs these creatures to balance once more

Cutting down forests will do us no good
It produces more carbon in exchange for some wood
The more people that come, the more land we take
For farming for feeding the people we make

Solutions abound, but the problems are greater
Not changing things now means much worse things later
So let's start with a story 'bout a stallion named Cello
One special horse, a remarkable fellow

Cello was wild and left free to **roam**
The Rio Grande River was the place he called **home**
From South Colorado to the Mexican **sun**
Cello and his herd of wild mustangs would **run**

Grazing and lazing from river to **plain**
All was in balance, 'cross their Rio Grande **range**
He loved the adventure that each day would **bring**
But a storm was coming that would change **everything**

Industries grew and needed more land
The mustangs were blocking some very big plans
Cello was worried and led the herd south
He couldn't understand why they were being pushed out

Life had become a whole lot less free
Wherever they went, there was less space to be
But what happened next, they couldn't have dreamed
Out of the sky came a giant machine

For hours the mustangs ran for their lives
Cello knew not if the herd would survive
The machine was relentless, wearing them down,
Wherever they turned, the machine looped around

Cello could see that the fences were closing
Up ahead, steel pens loomed dark and imposing
The mustangs were done, the end of a chapter
There was nowhere to run; the herd had been captured

The machine flew away, the steel gates slammed
They were locked in a prison and did not understand
Freedom abandoned, they gathered together
Cello now worried they'd be locked up forever

Months went by and turned into years
They longed for the plains and escaping this fear
More mustangs came, an entire horse nation
Cello was lost in quiet desperation

Over the years, the land had been changing
With megabeasts gone, life began rearranging
Each change rippled, and balance was lost
The environmental impact was starting to cost

The soil's now dry, and fires have increased
The long grasses withered, some species, deceased
There's an order to nature and a circle of life
The order has changed; the land is in strife

A team was assembled to discuss what to do
The best minds around were thinking things through
Intelligence was gathered from all around the globe
To share what had worked from people who know

They found out that wolves had been reintroduced
In Yellowstone park, they set the wolves loose
In the years that followed, the results amazed
Balance returned, fields were not overgrazed

The verdict was simple; they knew what to do
Rewild the horses, the whole mustang crew
To prove the results, they'd have to start slow
They would need to find land where the horses could go

Cows prefer flats, but horses don't mind
They can live on the slopes and be perfectly fine
But to give horses rights to be free to live there
Native citizenship had to be redeclared

A search was mounted to go nationwide
A search for a fossil to prove for all time
That the horse that is here is the horse that once left
And finally establish what rights they should get

The search was funded by Cana Foundation
The scientists set out for the horse's salvation
They were rather excited when they called up to say,
"Preserved in the dirt was ancient horse DNA"

Cello had a sense that something was up
After so many years, it was time for some luck
Land was located for a rewilding test
And the group thought that Cello's whole herd would be best

The next day a team, rolled up in trucks
The ramps dropped down and slammed in the dust
The pens sprung open, and Cello stepped forward
Within a few seconds, the whole herd were on-boarded

A short journey later, they rolled to a stop
The ramps dropped down and out the herd got
For a moment they stood, silently frozen
Not yet believing it was they that were chosen

Slowly with purpose, Cello stepped forth
It had now been ten years since the day they were caught
Altogether the herd took flight through the pass
Cello and his family were home-free at last

In the years that followed, the balance returned
The long grass came back, along with the birds
The soil remoistened, and the trees became green
Animals were now where no animals had been

They all had their place, and they all lived in peace
Rewilding had worked, all mustangs released
Lessons were learned, we discovered new ways
And that's why the mustangs run free today

Well, maybe in the future. For now, the mustangs
are still in cages, but Cana Foundation is working
on it. And our scientists really did find that fossil;
ancient genetic material buried in the ground
[sediment] in Canada's Yukon.

Scan the QR Code to see how you can help Cello
and his family at CanaFoundation.org

ABOUT THE AUTHORS

Simon E. Mills D.B.A. Author of 37 books including 18 children's storybook titles, ghostwriter for prominent biographical books for public figures including New York's 55th governor, David A Paterson, legendary drummer Liberty DeVitto of Billy Joel's touring and studio band on over 150 million albums sold, and many other prominent personalities. Dr. Mills' children's books are written in rhyming verse. The style has developed over decades as a professional musician and commercial music composer. He lives in Manhattan with his wife and children who try continuously to keep him from remaining a child.

Ross D. MacPhee Ph.D. Prior to joining the American Museum of Natural History as **Curator**, Division of **Vertebrate Zoology-/Mammalogy** in 1988, Dr. MacPhee was an Associate Professor of Anatomy in the Duke University Medical Center. He has also taught at Columbia, New York University, and several universities in Canada. Dr. MacPhee's research interests span the evolutionary history of mammals, island biogeography, and the biology and causation of extinction. He has led or participated in more than 50 scientific expeditions in 15 countries, including both polar regions. Recent fieldwork venues include Yukon, James Ross Group (West Antarctica), and Argentina. He lives in Manhattan with wife, professional archivist, Clare Flemming. Dr. MacPhee also serves on the board of Cana Foundation and leads the science advisory board.

Scan this QR code with your phone camera for more titles from imagine and wonder

Your guarantee of quality
As publishers, we strive to produce every book to the highest commercial standards. The printing and binding have been planned to ensure a sturdy, attractive publication which should give years of enjoyment.

Replacement assurance
If your copy fails to meet our high standards, please inform us and we will gladly replace it.
admin@imagineandwonder.com

Scan the QR code to find other
amazing adventures and more from
www.ImagineAndWonder.com